SUNDOWN DUDE

SUNDOWN DUDE

Bernard F. Conners

British American Publishing

Published by British American Publishing, Ltd.
19 British American Boulevard, Latham, New York 12110

Library of Congress Control Number: 2020947714

ISBN 978-0-945167-64-8

Printed in the United States of America

First Edition

Book design by Ron Toelke, Toelke Associates

Photos: Cover and interior photos by Stephen Simmons, Ken Ellis, and Monica Oberting

This novel is a work of fiction. Names, characters, places, and incidents are either the product of the author's imagination or used fictitiously. Any resemblance to actual events, locales, organizations, or persons, living or dead, is entirely coincidental and beyond the intent of either the author or publisher.

Chapter One

It was sundown, closing time at the Lexington Avenue branch of the Manhattan Savings Bank. From long, narrow windows high on the walls of the bank's spacious interior, yellow sunbeams flickered down, remnants of a fading day. Behind a barricade of teller windows, amid sounds of rustling paper and whispering conversations, employees tended to the day's closing and the safekeeping of the bank's cash. However, in the large customer area just beyond the barrier of teller windows, plans of a different nature were underway for the disposal of bank funds.

There, a solitary figure with a mustache and a small goatee, wearing sunglasses, baseball cap, jacket, and jeans, stood at a long customer table ostensibly attending to some final banking business. A discerning observer of the scene, however, may have perceived something a trifle unusual about the seemingly relaxed customer. Perhaps a slight trembling of the pen in the hand, or the light tapping of a foot against the leg of the table or the anxious shifting of the eyes behind the large dark glasses. After noting one of the last customers heading toward the exit, the figure breathed deeply, gave a quick glance about the room, picked up a small deposit bag from the table, and moved toward a teller's enclosure close to the front entrance where a young woman was completing her day's work. She looked up as the customer approached.

"Sorry, sir," said the woman, an expression of annoyance on her face. "This station is closed. You'll have to—"

"Won't take a minute," said the figure curtly, pushing a note under the window and glancing toward the adjoining teller's station a few feet away. "Just making a quick withdrawal. Make it quick so we can both get out of here!"

With a deep breath and sullen expression, the teller set aside a paper on which she'd been working and glanced down at the note. In large block letters were the words:

ROBERY

PUT 50 BENJIES IN BAG—$5,000

YOU GOT 30 SECONDS

The teller looked up quickly, the initial surprise and fright in her brown eyes replaced by a glimmer of defiance. Like most bank employees in the country she had been trained for such a situation. Bank holdups had reached epic proportions and financial institutions had concluded that it was more practical to cooperate with robbers and relinquish the cash rather than risk severe consequences such as bad publicity resulting from injury to employees or customers. Besides, losses were usually moderate, often less than a bad loan. Insurance covered most liabilities, which were minor line items on spreadsheets. Instructions to bank employees were sometimes exceedingly simple: "Just give them the money and get them out before someone gets hurt!" Indeed, some embittered tellers expressed the mordant feeling that robbers were now accorded the courtesy of customers making withdrawals.

It was not the case with the present teller. An independent young woman with a stiff backbone, she was less intimidated than some of her colleagues might have been. There was something about the figure confronting her that she would not have expected in a bank robber. Something far less threatening, callow, even becoming. Perhaps his manner of delivery or his facial hair . . . yes, it seemed unusual. Also, he reminded her of an article in the paper that she'd read a few weeks before about a person who had held up banks just before closing. It described the robber as neat and rather young and labeled him the "Sundown Dude" because he committed robberies late in the day.

After a brief glance at the note, she pointed to the paper: "Look, you misspelled robbery. There's two b's in robbery." Mostly to herself, she murmured, "No wonder he's robbing banks. He can't even spell!"

"What?" exclaimed the robber. "Listen, sister, I didn't come in here for a spelling lesson. I spelled it phonetically so a dummy like you would understand. Now, I want fifty Benjies in a hurry, understand? Put 'em in this bag!" The teller jumped back as the deposit bag was shoved at her. Concealed by the bag but protruding from one end was the dark muzzle of a small Glock 19 semiautomatic pistol. "You got thirty seconds!"

The sight of the muzzle pointed at her chest brought a sobering compliant expression to the face of the teller. "Okay, okay. But what's a freakin' Benjy?"

"Jesus Christ, lady. How the hell did you ever get this job? It's a hundred-dollar bill! Benjamin Franklin's picture's on the bill, dummy!"

"Okay! I get it! But I don't have fifty—what do you call 'em. Want me to ask my supervisor for—?"

"Look, stupid, give me whatever you got then!" said the robber, tapping the muzzle on the counter with frustration.

"Okay, okay! But I'm not stupid," said the teller, shuffling stacks of bills in front of her and shoving them across the counter. "Here," she mumbled. "Compliments of the Manhattan Savings Bank."

"Oh, thanks. Now, how about a smile?" responded the robber sardonically, adding, "You deserve a tip," and dropping a twenty-dollar bill from the money on the counter. "Buy yourself a margarita!"

The ensuing pithy response from the teller was not one found in the bank's training manual. As the robber moved toward the exit, the teller ducked down behind her counter, leaving one hand up cautiously pointing towards the departing figure, middle finger extended.

An elderly customer headed for the exit posed a slight obstacle. Displaying an unusual athletic agility, the robber spun around the woman to the door, glancing back briefly into the large customer service area. A flurry of activity was unfolding around the tellers' stations, wide-eyed individuals staring after the fleeing robber. The rest of the room was very quiet, beams of light from the long windows near the ceiling now diminished—the sunless scene preferred by the Sundown Dude.

Chapter Two

Once outside the bank, the figure was immediately engulfed by the surge of late afternoon pedestrian traffic that streamed down Lexington Avenue. Contributing to the sluggish mass of humanity were lines of virtually motionless cars propelled by little more than idling engines and mostly idle gas pedals. The immersion in the crowd helped provide concealment from possible exterior bank surveillance cameras, another reason the robber chose the evening hour.

A quick turn onto a side street headed west gave relief from the throng of people. Here, a deft move of the robber's free hand removed an artifice of beard and cap, releasing a tumbling length of blonde hair. The result was a striking transformation from nondescript bank robber to Charlotte Baxter. Pausing briefly, she stuffed the disguise and the bank deposit bag into a small shopping bag.

She had walked but a short distance when she heard the forlorn wailing of police sirens mixing with the nearby Manhattan traffic. "Probably a response team," she thought, "heading to the bank." The sound engendered a mixture of both concern and relief—a wariness of the rapidity with which the authorities had responded through heavy evening traffic, combined with a profound sense of satisfaction at having successfully performed her third bank robbery. She knew she was engaging in a dangerous and unethical practice, but the thrill of the adrenaline rush and the financial rewards it produced overcame her inhibitions. Robbing banks could become addictive.

After a toss of her head and quick ruffle of hair she adjusted her jacket and entered a small cafe midway down the block. Sitting at a counter near the door was a young man in his late twenties, whose face brightened upon seeing her.

"Charlotte," he said, rising exuberantly. "I was afraid maybe you'd forgotten me."

"Sorry I'm late, John," she said, walking toward the counter. "Got held up a bit at the library."

"Oh, that's okay. How about a drink?" he asked.

"Would it be okay if we got my bike first? It's over at that place on the West Side. I was supposed to pick up

Tommy at school after his baseball practice. I can drop him off at home and then go to dinner—or eat at home if you like."

"Sure, it's only five-thirty," said John, dropping change on the counter to pay his check. "My car's just down the street. Here, let me take that," he said, reaching for her bag.

"It's okay," said Charlotte, shifting the bag protectively to her other hand and moving toward the door. "I need the exercise."

John Rodgers was a man in love, but clearly out of his league. At five feet seven with brown thinning hair, glasses, and common features, he presented an acceptable appearance, but manifested a diffident, self-effacing manner perhaps more characteristic of a loving brother than a confident suitor. It was the demeanor of a man in love with a beautiful woman, who realized he was in far over his head, both literally and figuratively, and that his romantic affair could end abruptly with a hapless move.

Their association had begun some six months previously after a chance meeting in a Manhattan restaurant. It was because of John's tenacity that the relationship had evolved into a romance for him, but was little more than a matter of convenience and companionship for Charlotte.

With such an association that required him to be compliant, if not sycophantic, John was constantly on his toes—indeed on his tiptoes when Charlotte appeared in her stiletto boots—and there were times when he felt himself something of a flunky. But such thoughts were tolerable when dating a creature who dominated his romantic aspirations.

The ride crosstown was a relief from the traffic on Lexington Avenue, and they were soon pulling into an out-of-the-way parking garage that housed Charlotte's bike—a gleaming Harley-Davidson motorcycle that, combined with its striking driver, could prove a distracting traffic hazard. Indeed, the company had offered her a discount on the bike's purchase price, as well as a promotional fee for photographs. John had been considering a more modest Harley, one that he could afford and that would still enable him to keep pace with the fast-moving love of his life. It would require some heavy lifting with his moderate income as an editor at the *Paris Review*.

"I'll see you at seven-thirty," said Charlotte, after discreetly stuffing accoutrements into one of the saddlebags and climbing onto her bike. "We don't have to go out. It'll be kind of late. We can eat at home with Tommy, if you like."

"Sure, but I already made a reservation at—"

"Whatever you want," said Charlotte. After a cursory glance over her shoulder at an approaching car, she rolled out of the parking lot toward an up ramp at a nearby freeway, aggressively cutting off and irritating an approaching driver in the process. Here she was held up momentarily by crowded lanes, people resignedly waiting their own turn to enter the thruway. A slight twist of her wrist on the throttle brought a burst of speed enabling her to squeeze into one of the lanes ahead of annoyed drivers who were slightly mollified by the sight of the dazzling figure.

John sat in his car, uneasy as he watched the departing figure on the bike turning heads. His tenuous relationship with a beautiful divorcée and her seven-year-old son could fade quickly, leaving him with little more than a redolence of perfume and exhaust.

Chapter Three

Twilight. A darkening horizon streaked with rose-fringed clouds threatened the ball game underway in front of the elementary school where Tommy Baxter waited to be picked up by his mother. A tow-headed seven-year-old, he was among the smallest in his class, but perhaps one with the largest ambition—an avaricious genetic trait shared with his mother. Although a child, he already had aspirations to become a pitcher in the major leagues, most likely with the New York Yankees. It was just such a dream he was pursuing while waiting for his mother. A bored teacher sat impatiently behind a window waiting for the last of the children to be picked up.

Crouched, glove in hand, in front of a large wall near the entrance to his school, Tommy was engaged in an imaginary game in which he threw a battered ball against the wall and caught rebounds. If he caught a rebound safely, it was an out, but if he dropped the ball or the rebound went past him, it was a base hit. It was a game he played relentlessly while waiting for his mother on her motorcycle, which was often. Although he enjoyed the game, his love for his mother bordered on delirium. Each muffled growl of an engine, every sputter of a motor, no matter how distant, caused a skip in his heart. She was on her way. Suddenly, a burst of an engine accelerating came from a nearby open road. He knew the rumble and it caused an immediate flutter in his stomach. No question: she'd be there in a minute.

He'd have to hurry with his game. Two men on base and only one out. He'd try a curve. Look for a double play to end the game. The windup, the pitch. Then all at once over the top of a rise in a nearby road, the dazzling sight of a Harley-Davidson bearing a stunning woman, blonde hair curling from beneath a black helmet. His pitch was wild, of course. Two runs scored. The game was over, but who cared? His day was complete. Jumping to his feet, he rushed to the curb where the bike now lurched to a stop.

"Hi Mom," he squealed, jumping up and hugging her tightly, his eyes gleaming with expectation. He pushed his nose under her helmet, sniffing the familiar scented hair fused with exhaust fumes. He cherished the odor and intimacy, and squeezed his mother's neck as tightly as small arms would permit.

"Hey, easy, Tommy," said his mother, gently disengaging and reaching for a child's helmet on the passenger seat. "Here, put on your hard hat. John's picking me up for dinner in a little while."

"Oh, Mom," he said, disappointment clouding his face. "Not again. We were supposed to play cards tonight, remember?"

"We'll be home early, don't worry. Here, put your glove in the saddlebag there and get your helmet on."

A divorcée who had disengaged from a violent and abusive husband shortly after marriage, Charlotte Baxter was an independent woman unconcerned with social improprieties. Since childhood she had displayed an unusual ability to handle challenges many women would have found daunting, and often with an indifference toward the consequences for her adversaries. Such personality traits engendered only cool relationships and contributed to her reputation among the biking crowd as a "dazzler, but hands off."

At a young age she had become aware of the importance of money. Her father had died when she was young, and there was little money for her and her mother. This combined with a premarital pregnancy had caused her to forgo a small scholarship as an English major and writer at a state university after only three years. It was a decision that had disappointed her admiring teachers who had urged her to apply to Mensa, the exclusive international high IQ society, and to pursue a writing career.

Her marriage, an enormous mistake resulting from the pregnancy, had left an indelible mark. One of the few things she had ever heard her husband say worth remembering had been, "With money you're somebody, without it you're a bum." She'd left him before their son was a year old, severing all contacts and forgoing tenuous benefits that might have accrued to her through tortuous legal proceedings. Just the thought of financial dependence on him giving him any control over her made her shudder.

Having had only meager funds since an early age, she was inevitably governed by fears of financial instability. Of continuous concern was the need to provide for future requirements for her son. Clothes, education, medical bills were all challenges for which she had to prepare.

After reading about the rising number of bank robberies in the country, she marveled at the apparent apathy with which banks relinquished their funds. When she had to visit a neighborhood bank to deposit money from the fine collections of the library where she worked, she couldn't help thinking of robbery, and articles she read made it seem so easy. Almost like making a withdrawal. What followed had been predictable for an unusually bold intrepid personality. Three bank robberies. Not only had it provided financial rewards, she had grown to appreciate the excitement and drama that the practice entailed. And, of course, as an aspiring writer in college, she began to envision prospects for a book.

Extensive reading about bank robberies in newspapers and on the internet had enhanced her knowledge and skills. She had seen reports where many bank robbers had continued to rob banks for the thrill involved long after the possible consequences far outweighed risks and the financial results. Although she rejected the thought of possible addiction, it had come to the point that just entering a bank on normal business matters could inspire an inexplicable thrill. Now, gathering speed on her motorcycle, her young son's arms wrapped tightly around her waist, she experienced the exhilarating aftermath of her successful robbery that day.

"Faster, Mommy!" squealed the young voice on the rear seat. "Faster!"

With a slight rotation of the throttle on the handlebar she increased the speed, feeling the brisk wind on her face beneath the goggles. With her left hand she reached across her midriff to squeeze a small arm affectionately. The move caused a slight swerve in her bike, a momentary disorientation that was dangerous. But she was accustomed to the risks. Such recklessness had been part of her life. It was in her blood.

"Riding my bike is great therapy," she thought. "Particularly after a bank job. It blows away the butterflies."

Thoughts of her impending evening with John engendered mixed emotions. He'd made reservations at a Manhattan restaurant, and would be disappointed to stay home and play with Tommy. But it would be expensive for John to go out. Salaries at publishing houses were moderate and while she had offered repeatedly to share dining expenses, he had been adamant about paying. Accustomed to his attention, she was well aware of his desire for a long-term relationship, and rebuffing his physical advances without hurting his feelings could be challenging at times. But thoughts of another marriage had stiffened her resolve. The only future male kinship in her life would be Tommy.

Chapter Four

John Rodgers hung up the phone, disappointed but not at all surprised. He had planned the dinner for two at one of Manhattan's upscale restaurants, an evening that could have cost much of his weekly income, depending on how many cocktails Charlotte ordered, and whether she had an appetizer or dessert. Even if he'd skipped the dining room captain's gratuity and fudged a bit on the waiter's tip, it still would have been a sizeable hit on the Rodgers budget.

Therefore, it was with a combination of relief and moderate disappointment that he reflected on the call that asked him to pick up some fast food for dinner and expect cards at home with her son Tommy. There was a downside. Since it was a Friday night, Tommy would be able to stay up later than usual, which would cut into any intimate interludes. Not that the latter was ever more than a little hand-squeezing or a hug that would assure him of a return engagement. But that was okay with John. Anything, even a pat on the cheek, offered the possibility of an exciting future.

John was at the apartment precisely at 7:29. He was never earlier than the appointed hour. Charlotte was specific about time. He had learned the hard way—once appearing early for a date and finding himself standing awkwardly in front of her door for several minutes.

"Oh, hi John." The ravishing figure answering the door was still in a bathrobe when he arrived. "Would you mind picking up some papers for me at the library? I need to have them read by morning."

"Of course, dear," was the compliant response. "Where are they? At the front desk?"

And so it went. Errands, chauffeuring, menial tasks. . . . But for John Rodgers it was all acceptable. In a matter of minutes he would be back in the apartment with the most captivating woman of his dreams.

He completed the library trip and was back at the apartment shortly. This time, Tommy answered the door and the ambivalence about sharing his mother with John on a Friday night was apparent in his face.

"Hi John. Come on in. Mom's still getting dressed, but

we can watch television if you like."

Tommy was comfortable with his mother's suitor. It probably wasn't as good as having a dad, but having no recollection of his own father, he could only imagine what a father should be. Sometimes he envied his friends whose fathers took them to ball games. But that was all right. John seemed interested in baseball and he'd already converted him from the Boston Red Sox to the New York Yankees. Still, he was unsure about the future. His mother seemed to like John but what if they ever got married? Where would that leave him? One of the boys in his class had no mother or father. His mother had remarried and moved to California and the boy had to live with some relatives. Tommy thought of bringing up the subject with his mother, but she never seemed inclined to talk about boyfriends. That was okay. He liked John—particularly the new baseball glove John had given him. Besides, he wasn't sure, but he didn't think his mother would ever marry John. He didn't know why. In fact, he could never really understand why people got married.

"Sure, let's watch some TV. Maybe there's a ball game on," said John, taking an easy chair in which he often sat while waiting for Charlotte. "Are the Yankees playing?"

"No, not tonight," answered Tommy, turning on the television. "Tomorrow night."

"We'll have to go to a game one of these days," John said.

Tommy never believed John when he said that. He knew the only chance John would go to a game would be if his mother went, and that was a chance he estimated at a zillion to one.

"How are my two boys?" came his mother's voice breezing into the room. "How about some cards?"

"Oh, great," responded Tommy exuberantly, standing and moving quickly toward a card table in a far corner. "I was afraid you might be going out. Can we play pitch?"

"Sure, pitch is fine," said Charlotte. "How about it, John? You ready for some pitch?"

"Of course," replied John, trying to suppress his disappointment as chances of any privacy with Charlotte began to fade.

Sensing her suitor's letdown, Charlotte turned toward her son and said quietly, "Remember, Tommy, nine o'clock. Bedtime!"

"But, Mom, it's Friday night and it's already—"

"Okay," replied Charlotte, "nine-thirty. But that's it!"

Jumping from his chair, Tommy rushed to his mother, hugging her legs tightly. An additional thirty minutes was big time in the life of a seven-year-old. "You're the best Mom. I love you so much!"

John sat quietly watching the loving exchange, wondering as he had done countless times how he could fit into their future. He thought Tommy liked him, but he sensed a reservation toward him from the youngster, perhaps a vague concern for his own future should his mother get married. But that might just be a natural emotion for a seven-year-old.

Although Charlotte was loath to speak about her previous marriage, John sensed there had been no contact whatever between the boy and his father, and no indications there ever would be. What role John Rodgers would have in their future was incomprehensible. But as an editor he had spent much of his life reading and writing about love affairs, most of them, it seemed, fraught with heavy-hearted themes. He was well aware of the unpredictability of romantic attachments.

Chapter Five

One o'clock, raining, and bundles of leaden clouds tumbled low overhead. The dreary day contributed to the low spirits of the young woman sitting astride the Harley bike in Upper Manhattan. The exhilarating rush she normally experienced while anticipating a bank job seemed absent, so much so that she had started to consider a postponement.

A rainy day, fewer people to blend in with. A feature in the *New York Gazette* on rising bank robberies had mentioned the Sundown Dude. . . . Although the article had been sparse on details and had described the Sundown Dude as older, bigger, gruffer, more masculine than she, it was still a source of concern. So much so that Charlotte had moved up the time of her robbery and modified her outfit to include a man's raincoat, jacket, shirt, and tie. But was it enough? Was she pressing her luck? The questions continued to mount as she sat on her bike contemplating the robbery.

But she had to proceed. She'd taken time off from her job, John had agreed to pick Tommy up from school, and she'd spent time casing the bank. The Westchester Savings and Loan seemed a logical target. There was no apparent guard, at least not in uniform. Yet, you never could be sure. Because of the increase in robberies, banks had increased security; she'd read that even some bank managers now carried weapons.

But it was time to move. With the rain her umbrella offered some protection from the high quality image security cameras. She'd located a place for her bike a block away in an unobtrusive spot behind a large truck near an on-ramp to a thruway—a preferred arterial after a robbery. She'd be lost among many cars before police responded. Chest throbbing, she slid from the Harley and headed for the bank.

At the entrance she paused briefly, feeling with her elbow the pistol tucked securely in the bank deposit bag in her pocket. A quick motion with her hand assured her the facial hair was in place. She realized she was now probably on a surveillance camera and nonchalantly pulled her cap low over her brow. With a final breath, she pushed through the door.

Once inside, initially she was concerned by the lack of customers. Fewer bodies to meld in with. A glance about the room revealed nothing different from what she had seen the previous week when she'd cashed a fifty-dollar bill while casing the premises. Everything seemed the same, including the row of teller windows with the young woman in the station next to the entrance. However, the teller looked younger than she remembered. After pretending some banking business at the table, she took the small note she had prepared from her pocket and moved toward the teller.

"Robbery!" said Charlotte, lowering her voice to a gruff masculine pitch and pushing the note under the window. "All your hundreds!"

Startled, the young woman glanced up quickly, and then lowered her eyes to the note:

ROBBERY

ALL YOUR HUNDREDS

30 SECONDS

The face peering from behind the window, frightened at first, then softened. "Of course, sir," she said with a wisp of a smile. "How would you like your hundreds, in twenties?"

"In hundred-dollar bills. Benjies! Read the note! Can't you read?"

"Oh, yes," came the compliant response, remorsefully. "I'm sorry, I was a little nervous," she said, reaching for some bills in front of her and shuffling them. "I don't have many hundreds; would you like some fifties?" she added accommodatingly.

"Yeah, all your fifties," said the robber, now less gruffly, relaxed slightly by the teller's apparent cooperation and gracious manner. "But hurry up, this is a robbery! You got twenty seconds!"

The teller continued bundling the bills and then, her young face seemingly more relaxed, looked up and smilingly said, "I probably shouldn't ask, but are you the Sundown Dude?"

"The what?" said Charlotte, looking at her, startled. "Are you serious?" Then, flustered, adding, "How could I be the Sundown Robber? It's only one o'clock!"

"Oh, sorry," said the teller, apologetically. "I just thought you might be the Sundown Dude. You kind of looked like him from his description in the *Gazette*."

"Look, young lady. I'm not the Sundown Dude, okay? Just tend to your business and fork over those Benjies."

"The what?"

"The hundreds, for Christ sakes! Look, I gotta get outta here. Give me the f-----g money!"

Rebuffed, the teller was quiet for a moment shuffling the bills, then stacking them on the counter in front of her. "Here," she said, pushing the bills toward Charlotte. "That's all I got, but I'll tell you something, mister. I still think you're the Sundown Dude. You know, your beard, the way you talk. You don't sound like a robber. . . . I'm sorry, mister, but I think you're the Sundown Dude."

"Sundance Dude?" said the teller next to her, now interested in what was happening in the adjoining station. Leaning toward her colleague's counter, she said, "Did you say Sundance Dude?"

"Not Sun*dance*, Sun*down*!" corrected the younger teller.

"I told you, I'm not the Sundown Dude," injected Charlotte, now frustrated, breaking into their conversation. "What the hell's the matter with you people. Can't you understand? This is a freaking robbery—a holdup! Don't you—"

"Any chance you'd give me an autograph?" interrupted the younger teller, emboldened by the other teller's involvement, and holding onto the cash in front of her.

"What? Are you crazy?" exclaimed Charlotte, reaching for the bills. "Can't you get it through that crazy little head of yours, I'm not the Sun—"

"It won't take a second," interrupted the teller, pushing over a pen and a small piece of paper. "Just write an SD like this," she said, demonstrating.

"Oh Christ," said Charlotte disgustedly, grabbing the pen and scratching "SD" on the paper. "There! Now give me the f-----g money!"

"Could I have one too?" whispered the teller next to her, leaning across the counter and handing over a pen and slip of paper. "It's to Beatrice. Just say something like Best Wishes."

"Are you crazy?" said the robber, ignoring the request and flipping the pen from the first teller back toward her. "I'm outta here!" Taking the money from the counter, she backed away, making a last futile grab for the autographed slip of paper on which she had scratched the initials "SD."

Stuffing the bills in the deposit bag, she moved toward the door. Once outside she headed briskly for her bike. With a moment to reflect on the banking episode, she saw it was ridiculous to have written the initials "SD" on the teller's notepad. It was hard evidence; for all she knew it was DNA evidence. But it had been a foolish split-second decision made to get the teller to cooperate. She hoped it would be of little significance.

But she definitely had to change her method of operation. The press was homing in on "Sundown Dude." Maybe she should change her disguise. Possibly revert to a woman wearing sunglasses, wig, and high heels. Of one thing she was certain. The *New York Gazette* loved stories like this. They'd created the Sundown Dude and would feature it whenever they could, regardless of the facts. That was the nature of a tabloid: they'd wring every last penny out of their investment. Thoughts of an upside had begun to crystallize, however. Such articles were wonderful publicity for a nonfiction novel. And it had occurred to her—what a great character for a book. It might even be a best seller and the royalties could help secure Tommy's future. . . . In effect, the *Gazette* was giving her free advance publicity for the book. Absorbed in her new dream, she imagined providing for her son while furthering her own writing career.

Within a few minutes she had reached her bike near the on-ramp to a thruway. Quickly removing the facial disguise, she mounted her Harley and started up the ramp to the heavily traveled road. She was about to move onto the thruway when she noticed a closely following SUV. The driver pulled up alongside her on the right, slowed down, and lowered his window.

"Nice Harley," said the driver, a man in his mid-thirties with a pleasant smile. "I've got a Harley. Where'd you get yours?"

Always an object of attention on highways, Charlotte knew the danger of roadside encounters. After a polite tip of her helmet, she nudged the throttle on the handlebar, and in a burst of speed and exhaust was off into an adjoining lane.

She had traveled but a mile or so when she saw a formidable sheet of driving rain beating the pavement ahead. A distant overpass appeared to offer some protection on the side of the road. With rain beginning to pelt her face and helmet, she slowed, looking for shelter under the viaduct. Once under cover, her thoughts turned to the driver in the SUV who had tried to engage her in conversation moments before. Her parking might cause him to stop and try to continue his overtures. With this in mind, she squeezed between two vehicles with female drivers that seemed to provide some seclusion.

After shaking water from her jacket, she opened a side pocket on her bike and discreetly examined the funds she had stashed in the deposit bag following the robbery. She was pleasantly surprised to see the slew of fifty-dollar bills among a few Benjies and smaller denominations. Quickly she closed the parcel and was preparing to leave when she was startled by a heavy masculine voice from behind the car next to her. She turned to see a tall pleasant-looking man with a wide smile standing nearby.

"Hi there," he said in a friendly voice. "I had the feeling you were trying to lose me back there."

It was the driver of the SUV. Well-dressed in a brown jacket and ascot, he presented an urban appearance, much more appealing than the impression she had received from their prior encounter.

"Oh, hi," she acknowledged. "Not at all. I found it a bit awkward back there with all this traffic."

"Of course," he said, retaining his smile, which was marred only slightly by a broken front tooth. "I imagine you get lots of attention on the road and have to be careful. Well, I won't hold you up. I just wanted to ask if you belonged to any bike clubs?"

"No, not really," she said, glancing over her shoulder at

the passing cars. "I'm a working girl. No time." She pulled on a glove, indicating her departure.

"Well, I'll let you go," he said. "I just wanted to mention . . . . I'm president of the Harley Club in White Plains. We're always interested in new members. Have you ever thought about joining a club?"

"No, not really. I don't have the—"

"We really have some nice features," he interrupted, moving closer. "Discounts on insurance, merchandise, rallies, all kinds of events. . . ."

"I'm sorry," said Charlotte, breaking in, and pulling up the kickstand on her bike. The rain was letting up, and she wanted to end this conversation. "But as I said, I'm a working girl. If I ever want to join a club, I'll call you in White Plains." Starting her bike, she began to back out. "I hope you understand," she said, delivering one of her irresistible smiles.

"Yes, of course," said the man apologetically, backing away and bumping into one of the adjacent cars. "Just thought I'd give it a shot. Always working. Just like you."

Once out on the road, Charlotte adjusted her visor and reflected on the meeting. He wasn't a bad-looking guy. But with all her experience she was good at assessing such contacts. And that was definitely a "tip the hat, see ya" situation. She'd already been to his club in Westchester. It was a nice place as bike clubs went, but she hadn't been that happy with all its members. One in particular engendered foul memories: her former husband.

The thought gave rise to a thrust of energy in the Harley and she flashed past several cars. In the distance, unfurling patches of blue skies displaced the clusters of purple clouds, promising a restful and rewarding sundown.

Chapter Six

SUNDOWN DUDE ROBS BANK
LEAVES AUTOGRAPH

"**D**id you see this?" said John Rodgers, holding the newspaper's headline up in front of Charlotte. "What's the country coming to? He robs a bank and leaves them an autograph?"

The Sundown Dude was now a celebrity and the lunchroom at the Lakeville Library in Westchester was heavy with foreboding.

"Oh, that's just the *Gazette*," said Charlotte lightly. "They sensationalize stories to sell papers, you know that."

"But there's a police report," countered John. "They got the guy's autograph from the bank. Don't you see? The robber gave them something they may be able to trace. Fingerprints. DNA!"

"Oh, I don't know," said Charlotte, her manner now

defensive. "He was probably wearing latex gloves. Those tellers gave him almost three thousand dollars. That was worth an autograph, don't you think?"

"Three thousand? It doesn't say anything here about how much the guy got. How do you know how much he got?"

"Oh, it's in one of those other papers out there in the library," said Charlotte, nodding toward another room, "C'mon, let's forget it. I've gotta get back to my job. Don't you have to go back to your office? Don't forget to pick up my laundry."

"I still think it's weird," said John, folding the paper. "Makes me think I should be robbing banks rather than editing manuscripts."

"Oh, well, so what?" said Charlotte standing, straightening her skirt. "You could always start robbing banks. Who knows? Maybe we could be a team like Bonnie and Clyde."

"Who?"

"Bonnie Parker and Clyde Barrow. Didn't you see that movie? They were lovers. Bank robbers back in the thirties. They even tried their hand at writing poetry about their robberies. Maybe they were on to something."

"Yeah? Well, I doubt if they were leaving their autographs at banks," said John.

"Maybe not. But they weren't reading manuscripts for a living either," said Charlotte dismissively. "Look at all those rows of books out there in the library. Most of them by writers who probably died broke. Makes me wonder why I bother writing." She got up to leave, and with a wave and a cheerful "Don't forget my laundry!" closed the door behind her.

As she walked past the stacks of books toward the suite of administrative offices at the front of the library, Charlotte noticed the branch manager, Harvey Wheeler, leaving his office. A tall, slender, balding man in his late thirties, Harvey had a reputation for displaying affection for younger women. When first applying for her position at the library, Charlotte was quick to discern Harvey's predilection toward young females. Her job interview had been completed quickly, notwithstanding her lack of a degree in library science, and she had soon found herself ensconced at a desk near Harvey's office door.

Although the propinquity of her new boss was challenging, Charlotte found some relief in the nearby aisles between book stacks that provided a means for evasion.

Later that evening, when John and Charlotte were having a cocktail at a nearby pub, Harvey's name came up.

"I've heard a lot of stories about him from other staff," said Charlotte. "He harasses women and gets away with it."

"Why don't they report him?" John asked.

Charlotte sighed. "Men think it's so simple, but it's more of a hassle than you think. If you've got a good HR department, which we don't at the library, you still have to file a complaint and tell your embarrassing story and then half the time no one believes you anyway since it's your word against his, and then you've made an enemy of the boss—that is, if you still have your job. Honestly, it's easier to just evade. You get used to it. You get good at dealing with it if it happens enough. I'd need a computer to count all the passes made at me. Particularly on the Harley. Sometimes I'm afraid to stop at red lights. I've had guys try to get on my bike."

"Really? You never told me that. What do you do when they try that stuff?"

"That's the advantage of a Harley. Real fast start," Charlotte said with a pump of her fist. "Leaves them back in the road."

"Well, let me know if Harvey makes any passes at you."

"He may," said Charlotte. "I haven't been here that long. I think he's trying to get to know me better, though. I do everything I can to avoid him." And, Charlotte thought, if her new plan worked, Harvey wouldn't be her boss much longer. "Incidentally, I didn't tell you, but I'm starting another novel."

"Another novel?" said John.

"I gave up on the last one," said Charlotte. "Maybe you could help with this one."

"Sure, I'd like to help. What's it about?" asked John.

"Bank robberies," said Charlotte without hesitation.

"Banks? What do you know about robbing banks?" said John.

"I read the papers. I could write about this Sundown Dude."

"That might be difficult," John said. "You don't have the knowledge. If you're going to write, write about something with which you've had experience."

"Well, who's going to read about a working mother or librarian? I was thinking of something like a nonfiction novel. You know, along the lines of what Norman Mailer wrote, or Truman Capote's *In Cold Blood*. I've read some of those books. In fact, I told you about stuff I wrote in college, working on the college magazine. You can't be an English major and not know something about writing. I wrote a short story in college about a jewelry theft that happened on campus. My professor told me it could be published. I think I have a good feel for the genre."

John thought that a college short story assignment and a nonfiction novel were two very different things, but restrained himself. "If you want to give it a try, I'll certainly do all I can to help you with it. My first advice is just do your research."

"I'm on it," said Charlotte with a smile.

Chapter Seven

"**B**ut why do you need a pistol?" asked John Rodgers, his brow wrinkling. "Guns make me nervous. What about Tommy?"

"I have a pistol safe," said Charlotte. "It's always locked up here in the apartment."

The two sat in the small living room of Charlotte's apartment discussing her plans to leave shortly for the pistol range where she practiced shooting. In her hand was the small Glock 19 semiautomatic pistol that she carried in a holster on her bike. The holster was made by the Harley-Davidson company so that it fit inconspicuously behind the seat of her motorcycle.

"Gives me a little comfort when I'm alone on my bike," continued Charlotte. "Kind of a security blanket."

"But you tell me it's never loaded unless you're on the range," said John.

"That's right, but I could always use it to scare someone away. They wouldn't know it wasn't loaded."

"Well, I guess you're right. You certainly attract attention on the bike. Particularly among that motorcycle crowd," he added, rolling his eyes, unintentionally.

"What's that supposed to mean?" said Charlotte, standing and shoving the pistol into a pocket of her jacket. "You don't like the motorcycle crowd?"

"No, I didn't mean that," said John quickly, sensing a dialogue he should avoid. "It's just that most bikers are men, and you know. . . . You've told me how you get attention. Oh well, let's forget it. Uhm . . . we having dinner tonight? I could come over at—"

"Maybe not tonight, John," she said, moving toward the door. "I have to finish some things for the library. Perhaps tomorrow."

"Sure," he said quickly. "How about Friday? I can make a reservation at—"

"Let's talk tomorrow," she said, cutting him off as she stepped out the door.

"Of course," he said, quickly. "Tomorrow then. I'll call in the after—"

The door closed on his words. Slowly he walked to a

nearby front window and watched as Charlotte put on her helmet, then pulled out the automatic, checking the empty magazine.

"God, she is beautiful," he thought, feeling a deep yearning that he sensed would never be consummated.

His thoughts turned to the apartment a broker had brought to his attention. It was not far from the library in Lakeville where Charlotte worked and would be perfect for them. He was reluctant to bring up the subject, however. He had mentioned the advantage of sharing a place to save on expenses several weeks ago and although she'd been cordial and curious, she was not exactly excited. It was more of a "let's wait and see" answer.

But John Rodgers was aware of his position. He was in a lopsided love affair with an enchanting woman from whom he had neither the strength nor the desire to disengage. And there was always the chance that Charlotte might decide to live with him. Although she rarely addressed the subject, he sensed from occasional comments her concern about Tommy growing up fatherless. As long as she continued to see him at all, he was firmly committed to their relationship.

He stood, ready to leave, when he glanced into Charlotte's bedroom and noticed a sheaf of papers near a computer on a desk. He wondered if it could be the start of the novel she mentioned. On a nearby table he noticed Truman Capote's nonfiction novel *In Cold Blood*.

Hesitating, he considered entering the room for a closer look—an idea he rejected after reflecting on the implicit trust governing their relationship. For him to enter her bedroom after she had left would be a flagrant invasion of her privacy. If she wanted him involved with her book, he would become aware of it shortly given the help he could provide as an editor. Besides, he was cynical about people starting to write novels. He questioned whether Charlotte would actually proceed with her writing endeavor. His professional life was replete with aspiring writers who never fulfilled their aspirations. Although she had worked on her student magazine in college, and had to write occasionally for her library job, he had seen nothing to suggest her ability to finish a book—particularly on a subject as alien as bank robberies.

Once again his thoughts turned to the papers in the bedroom. A quick look could answer many questions. Still gripped by uncertainty, he paused, looking through a front window. There was no sign of anyone in front of the apartment building. Finally, after a glance assuring himself that Charlotte had probably left, he made his way to the bedroom. He had entered the room and had picked up a sheet of paper from the desk preparing to examine it, when he heard footsteps approaching. Shocked and dismayed, he replaced the paper and moved quickly from the bedroom as Charlotte's frame filled the front door.

"Forgot my—" She stopped, frozen in the entranceway, her eyes darting from John emerging from the bedroom to the desk behind him.

John started to speak but remained silent. Words would not help. He recognized immediately he had been caught. She was too observant. He knew . . . she knew!

Chapter Eight

Tommy Baxter was crouched in front of the wall at Lakeville Central School, fielding relentless rebounds. His mother was already a half hour overdue, but he and a monitor watching from a window had grown accustomed to her late arrivals. His ears tuned to the sound of engines on nearby roads, he waited expectantly for the familiar rumble of the motorcycle. It was almost dusk by the time a black sedan pulled up to the curb behind him. Following a backhand stop of a rebound, he turned to see John Rodgers peering from the driver's window.

"Hi Tommy. Sorry I'm late. Your mother called me to pick you up an hour ago, but I was with an author. C'mon, get in. We'll get some dinner on the way home. Your mom said she won't be home till late."

Tommy's disappointment was palpable as he trudged toward the car. "Did she say what time she'd be home?" he said dejectedly, throwing his glove in the back seat as he climbed into the car. "She's supposed to help me with my homework."

"I don't think it will be too late," said John, consolingly. "I'll try to help you with it if I can. Better yet, there might be a ball game on. So how was school? Anything interesting going on?"

"Nope."

Tommy's eyes were riveted on the landscape, but his mind was with his mother, arms wrapped around her waist on the Harley. Suddenly, he spoke, "If someday my mom gets married, where will we live? Would we move somewhere?"

"Oh," said John, startled. "Maybe." John paused to ponder the question. Then, guardedly, he said, "Why do you ask, Tommy?"

"Well . . . I don't know. . . . But a boy in my class. . . . Well, his mother got married. . . . And he had no father, so his mom went away, and he had to go live with some uncle or somebody."

"You mean the little boy had to go live with some relative?" John thought there was probably more to the story but refrained from questioning him. "Well, that would never happen with your mother. You'd always be with your mother."

"Are you sure?" asked Tommy.

John hesitated for a moment. "Well, I wouldn't worry about that. I don't think your mother's thinking of getting married anytime soon." Then, reaching his arm over the boy's shoulder, he said, "But even if she did get married someday, she'd never leave you. She loves you more than anything in the world."

After a pause, John changed the subject. "Maybe we can play some cards tonight when your mom gets home."

"I don't think Mom will play cards. She's writing a book. Stays up late at night."

"A book?"

"Yep, I hear her every night," said Tommy. "Sometimes till late after I go to bed."

There was another long pause and then John said, "Did she tell you what kind of book she's writing?"

"No, not really. It's a make-believe story, I guess. She said I wouldn't understand it. It's for grown-ups."

John's further efforts at conversation met with only a moderate response from his passenger who had been anticipating a rollicking ride back home with his mother on the back of the Harley. But he had learned from previous trips that John's driving habits conformed to his conservative personality. From where he was sitting in the car, the youngster had a good look at the speedometer that rarely reached fifty. His patience was further strained as they closed behind a heavy truck that was groaning well below the speed limit. Tommy winced as he watched the dial slowly settle back to a comfortable thirty-five. But he realized it was not the driver's nature to pass an eighteen-wheeler on a winding road after dark. Were he with his mom on the Harley, he thought, by this time the truck would be a mere blip of dust in the rearview mirror.

With a reposing sigh, he settled back in his seat. Following a moment of silence, with a touch of whimsy he said, "How fast will this car go?"

"Fast?" asked John with a look of wonderment. "Hmmm . . . . Well, I'm not really sure. Not as fast as your mother's Harley, I know that. I've followed her with her bike on the thruway with my own car on occasion, and I can never catch up." Indeed, he wondered if he would ever narrow the gap between his quixotic dream and fast-moving girlfriend.

Chapter Nine

A nondescript bank, surrounded by the safeguards that she liked. Her bike was parked inconspicuously behind a nearby warehouse, only one traffic light away from a heavily traveled freeway. She had timed the traffic light at only twenty seconds, assuring a rapid getaway before the arrival of police response teams. Wearing a jacket, jeans, sunglasses, and a cap covering her blonde hair, she had spent a few minutes inside the bank, casing the interior while obtaining change for a large bill.

Once outside and away from the bank, she removed the cap, letting her blonde hair tumble around her neck. It was a pleasant fall morning. She planned to rob the bank in three days. She had checked the weather reports and the outlook was for steady rain, which was good news, allowing for an umbrella to help shield her from cameras.

Within a few minutes she reached the deserted passageway next to the warehouse where she had left her Harley. She was well into the alley when she noticed a dark form appear from nowhere and start to follow her. At first, she paid it only moderate concern, but as she increased her speed to reach the more lighted area at the end of the passageway, she noticed the figure pick up his pace, drawing closer.

Alarmed, she sought to calm her nerves. "Just my imagination," she thought. She was accustomed to attention from strangers. But this was different. It was an isolated place, affording little protection.

"Say, Miss," came a gruff, heavily accented voice, now close behind. "Could you help me with directions?"

"Sure," she muttered, now thoroughly frightened. Her thoughts turned to the pistol in the holster behind the seat of her Harley at the end of the alley. But it was still quite a ways. She felt the panic welling inside. Should she try to run? No he was too close now. She had to remain calm.

"Just up here in the light," she said, motioning toward the end of the alley and quickening her steps.

"Just a second," said the figure, moving closer, his arm now reaching for her shoulder, pulling at her jacket.

Desperate, she wrenched free and rushed to the end of the alleyway where her Harley stood glistening in the sunlight. The figure, now following quickly, seized her arm. A blow from the man to her neck sent her sprawling next to the bike. "Help! My God, help!" she screamed.

"Okay, bitch," yelled her attacker. "Have it your way." He pulled on her legs, a knife now in one hand.

Terrified, she reached toward the holster on her bike for the pistol. Fumbling, she grasped the handle, pointing the muzzle at her assailant's head. "Let go!" she gasped. "I'll blow your f-----g head off!" An empty threat but loaded with invective. Within seconds her attacker was gone.

Unnerved by the encounter, she struggled to gain her composure. Chest pounding, she shoved the pistol in the holster and mounted her bike. After a furtive look at her surroundings she quickly straightened her jacket and started the engine. Within seconds she was safely through the alley to the main street where pockets of people strode leisurely, impervious to the sound of the melee absorbed in the rumble of Manhattan.

She sat on her Harley recovering, watching the throng of people who passed only a short distance from where she could have been severely injured or even killed. She reflected on the hazards of life in Manhattan where trag-edy was ever close by. But that was New York. Where the action was. Not for everyone, of course, but she was a New York girl. For her it was exhilarating, the touchstone of her existence.

She flipped down her goggles, hit the throttle on the Harley, and burst from the passageway, rudely scaring a pedestrian, but leaving her own fright well back in the alley.

Chapter Ten

"**B**ut what were you doing in an alleyway? In that part of Manhattan?" John Rodgers was agitated. Having listened to Charlotte's description of her encounter with the assailant, he had launched into a lengthy reproval, to the annoyance of his listener.

"Let's forget it, okay?" said Charlotte, interrupting John's reprimand. "I don't want to keep reliving the bloody thing."

"All right, I'm sorry." John leaned back in his chair and took a sip of his coffee. The two sat in the commissary of the Lakeville Library during Charlotte's lunch break. John was about to enlarge on his apology when Harvey Wheeler appeared in the doorway.

"Forgive me for interrupting," said Harvey, following an imperious nod toward John. "Charlotte, would you kindly stop in my office when you're free. No hurry, dear." A quick glance at his watch served to nullify those last words, and he was out the door.

John was quick to offer an assessment of her boss following his exit. "I don't like that man at all. There's a shiftiness about him that I find disturbing."

"Really," said Charlotte, crossing her legs and leaning back in her chair. "I rather like him," she said in a teasing manner intended to provoke. "He's an attractive guy, sort of. Kind of reminds me a bit of Cary Grant."

"My God," responded John predictably, his hand now flat against his forehead. "There's no explaining a woman's taste. But I think you're just putting me on, aren't you?"

"I better go see what he wants," said Charlotte standing, picking up her purse. "He probably just wants to talk," she said, arching her brow.

"I'm sure," said John with a wry expression. "Those types of guys love to talk."

"What's that supposed to mean? He's the boss. He wants to talk, we talk."

"Oh, I'm sorry," said John defensively. "I don't even know him. How can I say? Only he seems a little chummy with you, for a boss. Does he call all of his employees 'dear'?

I've heard that he makes passes at the women employees sometimes."

"Why, John, I'm surprised you'd say that. Are you suggesting that he's flirting with me?"

"No, no," John said quickly. "But after all, you are attractive, and these older guys like to—"

"Well," said Charlotte, sensing her jesting remarks becoming tiresome, "Let's change the subject, okay? I think I can handle Mr. Wheeler. If not, there's always #MeToo," she added waggishly.

"Have you started writing that nonfiction novel you talked about?" asked John, mentioning her book for the first time since the incident when she had returned unexpectedly to find him standing in her bedroom doorway.

"Yes, I've done a few chapters," said Charlotte, pausing at the door. After reflecting on the bedroom incident she'd concluded that John would have had insufficient time to look at her manuscript. "Soon as I have a rough draft, I'll show you. Maybe you could help me get a publisher. What kind of an advance could I get?"

"Advance?" said John, surprised. "Might be nothing at all. Depends on a lot of things. Unpublished authors have trouble even finding a publisher. Even published authors are being challenged these days. Not like it used to be."

Charlotte smiled and nodded. She knew he was trying to prepare her for disappointment, but of course he didn't know that the *Gazette* was doing all her marketing for her, with its nonstop speculation about the Sundown Dude. "Maybe when you read it," she said, "you'll tell me whether you think it might sell. I feel pretty good about my chances."

"Just don't get your hopes up too high."

"I won't—I promise," she said with a solemn, obedient expression, and added, "I *am* doing my homework."

Chapter Eleven

It was the small average-looking bank she had inspected prior to the attack in the alley a few days before. Having spent time scrutinizing the location in anticipation of the robbery, she felt that while the funds derived would probably be less than from a larger bank, it would be a relatively easy, less risky job. She was mistaken.

Friday was the day she had chosen, feeling the bank would have increased its cash on hand to cover customers' paychecks and weekend activities. She was surprised, therefore, to see relatively few patrons in the main customer area. Also, her plan for the robbery in early afternoon to lessen comparison with the Sundown Dude's evening exploits was thwarted by an unforeseen early afternoon thunderstorm. Although the forecast had been for rain, it was a heavier storm than expected.

It was nearing five o'clock when, dripping wet, she

finally entered the bank. Walking nonchalantly while taking in her surroundings, she headed for an empty table opposite a teller's area near the entrance. Here, she proceeded with her practice of making out a spurious deposit slip while discreetly observing the room. The lack of additional people with whom she could blend in caused her some initial concern, but as she became more relaxed in the room, it seemed less relevant. After noting someone preparing to leave from the teller station near the entrance, she scribbled her message declaring a bank robbery on the deposit slip and moved toward the window.

"Robbery!" said Charlotte in a low, commanding voice, placing the grocery bag next to her feet and pushing the note under the window.

"What?" said the startled teller, a young woman in her early twenties. Hands starting to quiver, she picked up the deposit slip. "I'm . . . I'm terribly sorry, sir," she sputtered, holding the note at arm's length like some repulsive object. "I can't read this."

"It's a robbery!" snapped Charlotte. "Don't you understand? A f-----g holdup!" she added anxiously, glancing over her shoulder toward the office in the rear. "Give me all your hundreds. Hurry up!"

The teller, appearing near collapse, struggled to answer. "But, I don't have many hundreds," she whispered plaintively, reaching toward a stack of bills. "Only a few. We're just a little bank, you know. They always told us we were too small to be robbed, didn't they, Elaine," she said, turning toward a nearby teller for affirmation.

"Christ almighty!" breathed Charlotte under her breath. "Just gimme whatever you got."

Intending to free up both hands, she turned sideways quickly, and reached to drop her bank deposit bag into her grocery bag on the floor. As she abruptly bent over, the brim of her cap caught the edge of the counter and fell to the floor a few feet away. "Goddam!" she cried. She quickly snatched up her hat and turning back to the teller, grabbed the slew of bills on the counter. Shorn of her disguise, she headed for the entranceway.

The confusion that followed brought the female bank manager hurrying from her office, picking up the currency that she presumed a departing patron had dropped.

"Wait! Ma'am!" she called after the fleeing customer. "Your money! You're dropping your money!"

Charlotte, attempting to restore her cap, had had enough of bank robbing for one day. Blocking her departure at the exit door was an elderly man.

"Mayday!" shouted Charlotte, as she squeezed past the figure, involuntarily reverting to the international distress signal sometimes used by bikers.

Outside, the rain was continuing and there were fewer pedestrians to mingle with. She was unsure how much the weather would conceal her from surveillance cameras outside the bank. She had no idea how much money the aborted robbery had yielded. Probably much had been lost on the floor during her hasty departure. It had been a disappointing day that would culminate in a long, wet ride home on her bike.

As she walked in the rain reflecting on her current affairs, her thoughts turned to John. Perhaps it was time to think seriously about a partner.

Chapter Twelve

SUNDOWN DUDE A WOMAN

Headlines in the *New York Gazette* and the riveting copy that followed offered little corroboration that the Sundown Dude was a woman. The newspaper had created the sobriquet "Sundown Dude" and now that it was the core of one of the biggest stories in Manhattan, the *Gazette* editors were not prepared to forgo the ensuing journalistic laurels and revenue. Indeed, even the word "Pulitzer" was overheard floating in the newsroom. Never mind that there was little evidence to validate the essence of the story. The tabloid's reporters' insatiable craving for the sensational overwhelmed the more restrained hands of supervising editors. The presses were spinning, and an endless stream of print was piling up at newsstands. Top executives were inclined to be unreachable when troubling questions surfaced regarding the validity of some of the copy. It was, after all, a time when many papers were foundering, and journalistic standards were in precipitous decline. The average reporter's usual beat had been expanded and guided by a new mantra: "The hell with the facts. Give me something that sells!"

But contrary to the hype and exuberance revving up in the *Gazette* newsroom, the mood in the Lakeville Library lunchroom where the story was being discussed was exceedingly somber.

"So why do you care what's in the papers?" asked John Rodgers, legs crossed, sitting across the lunch table from Charlotte. "It's just another story. So what?"

"Oh, that paper sensationalizes everything," said Charlotte. "It probably wasn't a woman."

"Well, I don't know about that," said John. "The picture they got of the robber's back from one of the bank's surveillance cameras looks like it might be a woman."

"Oh, you can't tell anything from that dark, fuzzy picture. It could be an ape!"

"Naw, no ape," said John with assurance. "It was definitely—"

"Look, John," said Charlotte. "Can we talk about something else? Why are you so f-----g interested in that story anyway?"

"I'm sorry," said John, surprised by Charlotte's anger and raffish language. Why did she react so emotionally to the story? he wondered to himself. After a moment of tense silence, he said, "Ah . . . did you. . . ? That is," he fumbled. "Have you thought anymore about that apartment?" he asked hesitantly. Almost immediately, he sensed it was not an opportune time to have asked about sharing quarters.

"Oh, I don't want to talk about that right now," said Charlotte irritably.

Her thoughts and emotions still muddled by the close encounter she'd had at the bank, she realized she'd have to hold off on further robberies that had become an important part of her plan. Money was always a consideration, and the robberies had offered a temporary respite. She would probably have to ask for a raise in her library salary. It was presumptuous, of course, since she had been employed at the library for such a short period.

She was aware of the liabilities inherent in such a request. It was maddening for her to think that women had become such pawns for men. But with funds limited she had no choice but to consider all her options. And her options could well include Harvey Wheeler when it came to money—certainly when it came to her salary. She was unsure where such a meeting might go. It might lead to other things, Wheeler's reputation being what it was.

"It would be nice to discuss some of the issues with John," she thought. But John probably couldn't provide any significant help. And he was little more than an afterthought in her life—someone willing to provide assistance with the menial things without cost to her. She had tried to be clear early in their association that their relationship was strictly a friendship devoid of any amorous or financial implications, and John had appeared to understand. Yet his suggestion regarding sharing quarters to save money, although logical, had engendered uneasy feelings. How long he would continue with what she considered to be little more than a brother-sister relationship was uncertain.

And there was always Tommy to be considered. His lack of a father would become more challenging with time. He sometimes asked about his father, and although she had the answers right now, she realized the questions could become more persistent, the challenges more problematic.

Chapter Thirteen

The open book stacks at the Lakeville Public Library continued to offer Charlotte a sanctuary of sorts. Next to the public reading area, they consisted of narrow aisles with shelves on each side where librarians and patrons could select books of their choice. More importantly for Charlotte, the stacks were close to her desk that was next to Harvey Wheeler's office and provided a temporary refuge from her boss's increasingly friendly overtures. Although not a permanent solution, the labyrinth of aisles continued to offer some temporary relief when she was alerted to the fact that Harvey was prowling. Despite the fact that Harvey could locate her in the stacks if he persisted, Charlotte had become adept at slipping into adjoining stacks of books at the first appearance of Harvey. Although this was something of a cat-and-mouse maneuver, she continued to feel that it provided an occasional means of evasion.

It was a fresh spring morning when robust signs of rebirth were blossoming on the grounds of the Lakeville Library. Nor were all of the burgeoning signs of spring-time confined to the outer grounds of the building. Indeed, inside the library a touch of prurient vitality was evident in the steps of Harvey Wheeler as he emerged from his office in time to see Charlotte, dressed in a tight navy-blue sweater and matching polka-dot high heels, rise from her desk and walk toward the stacks. He was quick to notice her appearance—a bit different from her usual flats and slacks—and assumed she had an appointment outside the office. Slowing his stride, he waited until Charlotte had reached one of the middle aisles, disappearing inside the stacks. Pulling a small booklet from his pocket he adopted a business-like air and followed her into the aisle.

"Oh, good morning, Charlotte," said Harvey, feigning surprise.

"Morning, Mr. Wheeler," said Charlotte, turning toward her boss and delivering a glistening smile. "Lovely day, isn't it?"

"Yes, looks like spring is here," said Harvey, pausing near his employee, taken slightly aback by the seeming warmth in her greeting. Although always courteous, Charlotte's customary manner toward Harvey had been one of a distancing, hands-off demeanor. Harvey was quick to notice the difference, particularly in the rather intimate surroundings offered by the stacks.

"Are you enjoying your job?" he asked, moving slightly closer and placing an elbow on the shelf close to her ear. "I'd been thinking of having a brief talk with you to see if things were going well. I've been receiving very nice reports about your performance. Perhaps we could take a few minutes for a chat in my office to talk about—"

"Oh, that would be nice, Mr. Wheeler," said Charlotte. "I'm sure we—"

"Please, call me Harvey," he interrupted. "I dislike all this undue formality. I hope you understand." Harvey punctuated his remarks with a pat and slight squeeze of her shoulder which generated an emotional but well-concealed wince in the recipient. "Perhaps you could drop into my office when you finish up here," he continued. "There are just a few other things I'd like to go over."

But Charlotte understood—far more than Harvey realized. Her plans for a raise were underway and Harvey would have little reason for concern about "undue formality."

Chapter Fourteen

"I understand you had lunch with Harvey Wheeler yesterday." John Rodgers's eyes focused on the floor, avoiding Charlotte's response.

"Yes, I did. Is that okay with you?" asked Charlotte tersely. "He's my boss. He says lunch, it's lunch!"

"I was just curious," responded John, a note of regret surfacing in his voice for having broached the subject. "It's just . . . well, you seem to be spending more time with him recently . . . when I call sometimes . . . well, you seem to be in his office a lot."

"Listen, John, I don't want you calling me at the office so much, understand? It interferes with my work."

"I'm sorry," John said. "It's just that recently . . . well, I don't know, but. . . ."

"What time is it?" asked Charlotte, glancing at her watch and shifting back from the table where they'd had lunch.

"I've got to get back to work. I'll see you tonight, okay?"

"Yeah, sure," John said, offering a weak smile as he lingered at the table. "Seven o'clock okay?"

"Can you make it seven-thirty? I have to pick up Tommy later than usual." She didn't mention her five o'clock meeting with Harvey Wheeler.

A moderate increase in her library salary had been obtained, but it did little to offset the loss of bank revenue. Also, despite her efforts to conceal the blossoming relationship with her boss, she sensed a silken veil of awareness among her library colleagues. Harvey, a married man whose roving eye was apparent to his staff, did little to allay whispers, particularly when his office door was closed during meetings with an attractive employee. The increase in salary had been obtained easily. So easily, in fact, that it fostered even more adventurous and remunerative ventures in Charlotte's facile mind.

It was soon after a rendezvous with Harvey that John Rodgers mentioned the meetings to Charlotte. They were dining at a restaurant not far from Charlotte's apartment, and emboldened by a second margarita, John had decided to broach the subject.

"You know, maybe I shouldn't mention this, Charlotte, but the husband of one of the women you work with told me recently that your boss is something of a womanizer. We've talked about this before, but apparently it's more widespread than I realized."

"What, who told you that?" Charlotte punctuated her question by putting her margarita down sharply on the table.

"This has to be in confidence," said John, his voice wavering. "He made me promise I wouldn't tell anyone. It could affect his wife's job. I promised that—"

"Well, you have to tell me," interrupted Charlotte. "It's my job, too, you know. I won't tell anyone. What did he say?"

"Well, it's apparently worse than I thought. He said this guy Harvey makes passes at everyone; that he's one of those guys who can't control himself around women. He apparently inherited money from his widowed mother that enabled him to settle some confidential lawsuits with women. I presume you've heard much of this stuff from the office whisper mill, but I felt I had to mention it, so you'd be prepared if he made any, you know. . . ." John's voice trailed off as he sensed himself rambling into no man's land.

Charlotte was about to speak and then became silent as she sipped her margarita. "Yeah," she said finally. "I've heard a lot of that stuff in the office. I guess I should tell you something, John. I've been thinking about it for some time, but I didn't want to tell you. I was afraid you wouldn't really understand. But you have to keep it to yourself."

"What?" said John, now afraid of what he might hear. "You mean he—?"

"Quiet!" said Charlotte. "Just listen to me. You'll hear about it soon anyway."

"What?"

"Just be quiet and listen!" admonished Charlotte. "He made some passes at me. In his office. . . . I'm going to get a lawyer."

"My God!" exclaimed John, his handkerchief out, now dabbing his brow. "Did he touch you or anything? My God! Why didn't you tell me? Did you complain to HR?"

"Our HR department is terrible, John. They just want the trouble to go away. People who complain usually get transferred. How could I tell anyone? I had to get a lawyer to find out my rights. Don't you understand? I did get a lawyer. One of those women who handle stuff like this. I saw her on TV. She told me not to tell anyone, not even you. I've got to put it all down on paper for her."

"But you have to tell me everything," said John. "Lawyers cost money. I want to help you but—"

"Care for another margarita?" interrupted the waiter who had approached the table.

"Yeah," said John, not looking up. "Make it a double."

"No, no more!" said Charlotte, pausing briefly until the waiter departed. "Remember, John, you can't mention this to anybody. I'm not sure this lawyer will take my case. She handles these things on a contingency basis."

"On a what?"

"Contingency! You know, if we win the case, she gets paid her fee and I get money for damages—you know, emotional stress and all that."

"But . . . but what if you lose?" sputtered John.

"She won't take the case unless she's sure she'll win. She says defendants in these cases never go to court. They always settle. She won't take the case unless it's prima facie."

"I don't know," mused John. "Sounds terrible. What about your reputation? All that. . . ."

"It's not about me, John. Don't you see? I'm the victim. Could get a load of dough. C'mon, let's go," she said, picking up her purse and rising from the table. "I've got to write it all down for the lawyer so she'll have it tomorrow."

She reached for her glass and drained the remnants of her margarita. "C'mon, let's go," she repeated. "I've got a load of writing to do." She added with a droll smile, "How do you spell 'groping'?"

Chapter Fifteen

Charlotte had indeed seen a lawyer on television she thought might help: Anna Brown. As a bright student only a few years out of law school Anna was quick to see a niche representing women with sexual harassment suits. An attractive, if somewhat stern-looking person, her flair for the dramatic and her legal background gave her almost immediate success on television. By means of the medium she became proficient representing women who brought suits inspired by the #MeToo movement that was sweeping the country.

Charlotte's initial phone call to Anna in Manhattan was handled by a subordinate of the lawyer and was not encouraging. Ms. Brown was extremely busy and if Charlotte were inclined to persist, she should send a letter with the particulars of her case including customary background references. Furthermore, she should not expect a rapid—or any—response from Ms. Brown. It was a surprise to Charlotte, therefore, that she received a phone call from Ms. Brown within a few days.

"Would Charlotte care to come to Ms. Brown's office in Manhattan to discuss her case?"

Charlotte would, indeed, and an appointment was arranged for the following week at which time Charlotte explained in painful terms the "outrageous, in fact lecherous, attacks" by Harvey Wheeler.

Anna had listened sympathetically and even suggested transgressions that may have occurred in those dreadful trysts that perhaps Charlotte had forgotten or overlooked. Suffice to say that by the conclusion of their meeting, Anna had fashioned a four-star legal case worth a sizeable sum against the hapless Harvey. When Charlotte experienced misgivings about accusing Harvey of behavior she herself had instigated, her resolve was buoyed by Anna's righteous anger. She was simply saving other victims.

It was suggested that perhaps Charlotte might want to avoid the Lakeville Library while Anna had the usual preliminary discussions with Harvey's lawyer. In view of her charges against Harvey, her severance from the staff was anticipated. Anna, although making no commitments, was relatively sure that a confidential settlement could be achieved in short order.

"My God!" John Rodgers was less assured about the issue as he sat in Charlotte's kitchen, listening to her describe her meeting with the lawyer. "Where are you going with this thing? Lawyers cost money."

"I told you," said Charlotte. "It's mostly on a contingency basis. I have to pay her some money to cover her upfront costs, but—"

"Listen, Charlotte," said John, raising his hand in an uncustomary silencing manner. "This is a whole new ball game. We have no experience in such things. What about your job? The people you work with? The publicity!"

"Hey, listen, John," said Charlotte. "You yourself told me about Harvey being a womanizer and all that. . . . You helped me see he needed to be taken down. I thought . . . well, I just figured all bosses acted that way until I watched Anna on television and talked to her. Don't you understand? It's the right thing to do. I owe it to all the other women out there who've been victimized." Her voice raised, she almost believed herself.

"Look, honey. Let's slow down, okay? I understand how you must feel with this guy harassing you and all. I just wish you'd told me about this stuff sooner. Maybe I should talk to Harvey. You know, man to man. Try to settle this whole thing before it gets out of con—"

"John! Stay out of this," said Charlotte. "Let the lawyers handle it. Anna knows what she's doing. We may come out of this better than you think. Understand?" Her flinty blue eyes now fixed him with a commanding look. "Understand?" she repeated.

John was ambivalent. Having worked in the publishing business for many years, he had been exposed to several cases of male sexual harassment by colleagues and was sympathetic to the trauma experienced by young women. He took a measured satisfaction that a predator like Wheeler was being confronted. But he also knew how dangerous that confrontation could be when it involved men in powerful positions.

"Believe me, Charlotte, I know how difficult this thing will be for you. The loss of your job . . . the publicity. . . . And I'm glad to think that this character can be stopped from threatening women. But I'm concerned about the fallout for you."

"Well, I am too. Don't you see how hard it is for me? That's why women let these creeps get away with this stuff.

I've spent my life with men taking advantage of me. If I can do something that helps women, I'm going to do it. And if I can get a few bucks out of it, what's wrong with that?"

"How are things with your book?" asked John, foreseeing the need for a change of subjects. "You mentioned you'd like my help."

"It's coming along," said Charlotte. "I should have something to show you before long. It's taking longer than I thought."

"Of course," said John. "I'm impressed you're sticking with it. It's hard work. That's why I'm an editor and not a writer! Have you done an outline?"

"No," said Charlotte. "But I've done a lot of research, and I'm moving along with it. I've thought of an outline, but I don't think an outline works with my type of book. I can't be sure what's going to happen with my story line."

"Well, you mention the research," continued John. "What type of research are you doing? Are you reading other nonfiction novels to see how established authors handle their material and—"

"Oh, sure. Mostly newspaper articles though. I'll have a rough draft for you before long. I'm trying to come up with an ending. We'll see. I should have something for you to read pretty soon. I've been tied up a bit with a lawyer on this other thing with Harvey Wheeler and—"

"Excuse me, Charlotte," said John. "Please forgive me for interrupting." He hesitated momentarily as if unsure of what he would say. "I'm sorry to bring it up again. But I talked to one of our business lawyers, confidentially of course, about harassment issues and I learned quite a few things. The law is very unfair to women when it comes to harassment cases. It takes a great deal of fortitude and courage for women to confront these predators in court and they often have precious little to gain from it. A woman must have compelling evidence before initiating an action and she may well end up with a shattered reputation."

"I'm not worried about that," said Charlotte with a wave of her hand. "My lawyer says they always settle. They want to keep it quiet."

"Well, that may be so," said John. "But if the press gets ahold of it, it's a different story. The individual being accused is often a prominent person with the power and money to undertake malicious, covert actions to try to destroy the character and reputation of his accusers. These pernicious individuals will lash out at their adversaries with everything at their disposal, and it can be devastating for women. I'm not a lawyer, but I suspect there are few cases in court which are subject to more hyperbole, slander, and outright lies than those involved with sexual allegations. It's the subject of much emotion, and many have serious consequences for both the plaintiff and defendant. 'Such cases should never be undertaken without serious regard for the consequences,' says this lawyer. He's had a load of experience."

"But what are women supposed to do under the circumstances?" countered Charlotte. "Are we supposed to just sit and tolerate all this?"

"I understand," said John, interrupting. "I admire very much the women who have the courage to take on these odious characters, but I'm thinking of the toll it could take on you. I'm just thinking that often it requires the most intrepid spirit to sustain an action of this sort."

"Well, I understand what you're saying, but if he ever threatens me, I'll definitely drag his ass into court."

"Just remember, Charlotte," said John. "There will always be costs associated with such litigation, be they monetary or emotional."

Charlotte fired an exasperated glance toward the ceiling, finishing with a withering look at her suitor. "Look,

John, let's forget it, okay? I think I know what I'm doing. Just stay out of it, understand?"

John hesitated, remaining puzzled. But only briefly. The one thing he did understand was the limits of his influence on Charlotte.

Chapter Sixteen

Although already a prominent lawyer in the #MeToo movement, Anna Brown's press was not always flattering. Charlotte had done a dutiful background search, and had been surprised to learn that the rather sweet, understanding lawyer who had guided Charlotte through her preliminary legal trappings with "that predator Harvey Wheeler," was in fact something of a factitious personality herself. The percentage of counterclaims by defendants in Anna's suits was significant and indicative of the lawyer's aggressive approach. In addition, there was a malpractice proceeding in which the attorney had been criticized by one of her own clients. Charlotte also discovered that Anna had changed her last name from Brezinski to Brown. But most of her discoveries Charlotte had attributed to the contentious professional life her attorney had chosen, and had dismissed it all as part of the territory. It was natural that there would be combative litigation in such highly charged lawsuits.

Several uneasy days followed before Charlotte received a call summoning her to the attorney's Manhattan office where she found herself sitting with five elderly women waiting anticipatively for a meeting with the lawyer. The age and appearance of the other women prompted Charlotte to assume that the women were there for legal matters dissimilar to hers. Her own age and winsome appearance in the tweedishly clad grouping made her self-conscious. She sensed disapproving glances suggesting possible bias against her in their parched, withered faces.

Her thoughts were interrupted by a brusque announcement from a secretary behind a desk at the front of the room. "Ms. Baxter," snapped the woman, "Ms. Brown will see you now. Second door on the right!" The curt instructions were bereft of any amenities, but rather more the manner of a Manhattan cab driver who had just slapped down the meter.

Anna Brown barely looked up from her desk as she pointed Charlotte to a nearby chair. She wasted no time on civilities. "I met with Meredith Perkins, Mr. Wheeler's attorney, last week. Her office is just over there on Madison

Avenue. I know her pretty well—had a couple of cases involving her firm. She's a no-nonsense gal. I outlined your charges against Mr. Wheeler, and anticipated a quick settlement on the issues. I met with her in her office again yesterday afternoon. I'm afraid it didn't go well."

"Didn't go well?" said Charlotte, cocking her head to the side curiously. "I don't understand."

"They're contemplating a countersuit against you," said the lawyer. "This could get pretty ugly."

"What?" said Charlotte, uncrossing her legs, leaning forward anxiously, and recrossing her legs. "I don't understand. How in the world can they sue me? I'm the victim. They can't—"

"It happens," said Anna. "With all these suits, defendants are preparing themselves for counteractions."

"Why, this is outrageous," said Charlotte, bracing in her chair. "You know what happened to me in his office. I was the victim of sexual attacks. Dreadful personal attacks!"

"These things happen," repeated Anna, closing her file and looking at her watch. "We'll have to prepare a defense."

"A defense? Why? How in the world did I get into such a situation? What am I defending against?"

"Mr. Wheeler claims you tried to seduce him," said

Anna. "This could get pretty tough. I have a duty to inform you that this could get pretty bad, and *expensive*!" added Anna, again glancing at her watch.

"*Expensive*? But it's all on a—what did you call it—a contingency!"

"Oh, no, my dear. Not counterclaims. No contingency there. Could get *expensive*," she repeated in a firm voice.

"Well . . . this is ridiculous," responded Charlotte. "I may have to get another lawyer," she added, insouciantly, her voice dropping to her adversarial New York tone. "How can he suggest that I tried to seduce him? I was the victim."

"Well, if we go to court. . . ." continued Anna, hesitating. "We can find out for sure what they've got."

"What they've got?" said Charlotte, her voice rising. "What the hell could they have? It's my word against his, isn't it?"

"Well, we'll have to see," continued Anna. "It may be *your own* words against *you*. Can't be sure. I know his attorney pretty well and I don't think she'd mislead me. She claims they have evidence that you tried to seduce him—"

"What?" from the exasperated Charlotte. "What evidence?"

"Can't be sure till we go to court. We can find out everything at a discovery hearing. Her client says you tried to set him up. . . ." The lawyer rose from her chair indicating an end to their meeting. "That wouldn't be good. Claims he has tapes of your meetings in his office. . . . You know, recordings!"

"Recordings?"

"Yeah, she claims he recorded all your meetings."

Chapter Seventeen

"**I**t doesn't look good." Charlotte sat in the kitchen of her apartment, disconsolate after having given John Rodgers a mitigated version of the meeting with Anna Brown. "We may have to go to court," she said. "That could be expensive."

"But why?" said John. "Just forget the whole thing. Claim it was a misunderstanding or something and—"

"May not be that easy," said Charlotte. "I've already been billed by my lawyer for her initial costs. I'm going to need some money. Soon!"

"Money?" said John, shifting uneasily.

"Yeah. Just a couple of thousand," said Charlotte. "I don't like to do it, but I may have to tap one of my relatives again."

"Relatives? You mean the ones who've been helping you out the past few months? But you told me that you couldn't hit them up for any more—"

"Yeah, but I didn't figure on this happening. Don't worry about it," said Charlotte. "It's only a couple of thousand, and that'll be the end of it. I'll talk to my relative."

The relative, of course, was a Manhattan bank she'd visited near Anna Brown's office on Madison Avenue, shortly after her meeting with the attorney. It seemed an ideal target that included a garage for her Harley only a block from the bank.

"I could check on that apartment I told you about a few weeks ago," said John. "It might help to move in together to save money—until you get your feet on the ground. I could—"

"No, I don't think that would be necessary," said Charlotte quickly. "Let's just ride this thing out for a little while. Things will be okay in a few weeks."

"Sure, but if you need something to tide you over, just let me know."

John rose and slowly walked to the door, Charlotte following. Here they paused and Charlotte squeezed his hand. Noticeable, seemingly, was a new-felt warmth.

"Thanks for everything, John."

She watched him walking toward his car and felt a surge of affection, her mind absorbed with conflicting emotions.

She regarded John as a strong reliable friend. Often—more recently, actually—she had wondered if their relationship would ever evolve into a marriage. She had read of individuals who were not initially romantically attracted to one another who had fallen in love over time and had married. Perhaps it would happen with John. She had constantly worried about Tommy being fatherless and he liked John very much. She felt confident that he would make a good husband and father. She had even listed him on the "Emergency Contact" forms at school and her doctor's office. And she *was* growing older. It might even be nice to adopt a brother or sister for Tommy, if it came to that.

Her thoughts turned from marriage to the New York City Bank. She had liked the bank's customer service area, broad and deep, and what looked like the manager's office at the far end away from the teller stations. There were no signs of guards or surveillance cameras, although she realized that the usual security facilities would be functioning.

Anticipation of another bank job whetted her appetite, arousing the urge for the thrill of the danger and the possibility of reward. With such thoughts came the question of when to discuss her novel with John. So far, he had offered little encouragement.

He mentioned several times that it would be hard to find a publisher for an unpublished author. And he had been quick to explain that the literary magazine by which he was employed was primarily involved with erudition and poetry, and probably not an appropriate place for a submission. She wished she could tell him what a bombshell best seller she might have on her hands—but she had to wait. . . . At least until she could think of an ending.

Chapter Eighteen

Another bill from the Brown law firm arrived at Charlotte's apartment, this one by overnight mail. Charlotte's response that the bill would be paid within two weeks coincided with her planned visit to the "relative" and secured a brief respite from the attorney. But there were other dealings. The two weeks' severance pay she'd received from the Lakeville Library was depleted, and a gallant gift of one thousand dollars from John Rodgers had been used for rent and groceries. The funds from the "relative" were now essential and the date was looming.

It was a dark day with heavy grey clouds gathering above the modest quarters in Lakeville. Charlotte sat on the edge of her bed unloading the twelve brass bullets from the Glock 19 cartridge magazine. Within four hours she would be entering the New York City Bank, and while an unloaded pistol was helpful for controlling uncooperative bank employees, she was determined to avoid an accidental shooting.

Holstering the pistol, she walked to a bedroom window and gazed out at the gathering clouds. Although the forecast had been for overcast skies, no rain was anticipated. She had planned her activities at the bank for early afternoon to avoid comparison and excessive publicity with the sundown robberies. Checking the grocery bag in which she kept her disguises, she left her apartment.

It was on the parkway to New York that she heard the police siren closing rapidly behind her. Immediately she realized she was over the speed limit and pulled to the side of the road. She was joined shortly by a tall, rugged-looking state policeman.

"License and registration, ma'am," said the trooper, approaching and pulling a pad from his jacket. "Bit of a hurry this morning, aren't we?"

"Yeah, guess so," said Charlotte, pushing her goggles back and quickly thinking of an excuse. "I'm a little late for work," she offered with a dazzling smile.

"Yes ma'am," said the officer, returning her smile. "License and registration, please," he repeated.

Charlotte leaned over, pulling her wallet from a side

pocket. The trooper seemed a friendly sort and she had learned from female bikers that the best way to handle such situations was to engage in conversation.

"Lousy day for a ticket," she said, handing him her driving credentials. "Late for work and a ticket!"

"Sorry, ma'am," said the officer, another smile. "You know . . . that's my job. What's in there?" he asked, motioning towards the grocery bag. "Narcotics of any kind?"

"Oh, jeez!" exclaimed Charlotte, thinking of her pistol and her bank robber's disguise. She needed help, fast. "It's just my kid's laundry. Say officer, listen. Any chance you'd just give me the ticket and let me go? I work at a McDonald's," she lied. "If I'm too late—no job . . . no groceries . . . no rent. I could really use some help, officer." A tissue had surfaced and she dabbed at eyes as dry as a bone.

The officer hesitated, the wry grimace of a man familiar with children's laundry darkening his face. Slowly he returned his pad to his pocket. "Okay, ma'am. But you gotta slow down. I had you at over eighty back there."

"Oh, man. You're great—really great!" she exclaimed, with genuine enthusiasm. "You'll never know how much this means to me," she said, patting his arm. "Drop into McDonald's, I'll give you good treatment!"

"Yeah, sure," said the trooper, looking uneasily in both directions over his shoulders. "Just be careful, ma'am. That kid's gonna be out of luck with no mother!"

As the trooper disappeared, Charlotte sat on the Harley reflecting on her close call. An inspection by the officer for narcotics would have proved disastrous when she tried to equate the fake beard and Glock 19 with kids' laundry. The close call underscored her resolve that the robbery would be her last.

She was anxious about John's initial reaction to her book. He had seemed unimpressed by what she had told him thus far. Of course, she couldn't tell him yet that she was the Sundown Dude, but his pessimism with regard to finding a publisher who would offer her an advance was still disconcerting. Her thought was to repay the banks the $15,000 she had secured from the five robberies with the advance and royalties from the publisher. The robberies would be morally defensible in her own mind as research costs for her book. She had toyed with the thought that it might prove an acceptable theorem as a defense in court if necessary. If she could repay the money, it amounted to little more than bank loans if there were no criminal intent. It offered some palliative measure to a slumbering conscience rarely overburdened. She had prepared meticulous documents reflecting her intentions, and the assurance of repayment out of the proceeds from her novel. It would be handled anonymously to protect her from prosecution and when somehow the banks or law enforcement discovered her identity from the novel and initiated court action, it would doubtless increase the book sales and her royalties and help to bolster her case in court.

To Charlotte, with her penchant for thrills and excitement, this seemed a reasonable plan. She knew it might be hard to convince John, though, with his conservative nature. But that was the future. For now, there were things to be done.

Chapter Nineteen

Charlotte picked up the bank form from the customer table and scribbled numbers on it quickly, pretending to prepare a deposit. Although she had been relatively comfortable with her reconnaissance several days before, now with the actual robbery imminent, she was concerned. It was raining outside as she had anticipated, and the rain had reduced the number of customers. Indeed, there were only three people in the large room, two at teller windows. Also, the woman at the station nearest the entrance was not the same younger woman who had been there previously. The person there now had horn-rimmed glasses and a stern countenance and looked far more mature. In fact, the adjoining tellers close by seemed older than they were during her last casing. As she stood pondering the situation, she reasoned that perhaps it was better to deal with a mature teller who was trained to cooperate—at least they wouldn't ask for an autograph!

The customer room itself seemed more imposing than she remembered, with walls of large concrete slabs and a low vaulted ceiling conveying a feeling of security and impregnability. At the far end of the room were small offices which she assumed housed the bank managers. Standing just outside the entrance of these offices were two men, one in a suit who she presumed was the manager, and the other wearing workman-like clothes, suggesting perhaps an employee or customer. When the two men stepped inside one of the offices, she decided it was time. Note in hand with the deposit bag and pistol inside, she walked toward the teller closest to the entrance.

"May I help you?" asked the teller, her eyes remaining fixed on the work in front of her, her manner suggesting she was busy and not inclined to be helpful.

Surprised by the teller's cool reception, Charlotte dropped her voice and responded roughly, "Yeah, you can help me rob this f-----g bank," she said, shoving the note across the counter. "All hundreds and make it fast! You got twenty seconds!"

The woman looked up sharply. Without speaking

she reached for some bills on the counter nearby. Charlotte was immediately struck by the teller's manner—the cool unruffled demeanor of one who appeared to have the matter under control. Slowly, the woman began sorting the bills in front of her. Sensing a dilatory tactic in the woman's actions, Charlotte was immediately suspicious. Had the woman sounded an alarm? Possibly with her foot? Charlotte glanced toward the offices at the far end of the room where she had noticed the two men previously. They had emerged slowly from the office and stood hesitating, one looking in her direction. After conferring briefly, they walked slowly toward the teller's station where Charlotte stood.

There was no question. They'd been alerted. Charlotte moved abruptly from the teller's window, heading quickly toward the door. There were few options. She had to get out of the bank, even if it meant threatening someone with her unloaded pistol.

As she neared the door she glanced toward the two men approaching, the man in workmen's clothes pulling something from under his jacket. Must be a guard, she thought frantically. There was little time to act. As she neared the entrance, she turned slightly, now holding her pistol, hoping for time to reach the safety of the crowded street.

Two shots, almost simultaneous explosions, crackled off the hard walls. A driving force pitched her forward into the revolving door where she slumped, quite dead.

Chapter Twenty

It was bottom of the ninth at the wall in front of Lake-ville Central School, where clusters of dark clouds drift-ed low overhead, remnants of a foggy day. Tommy Baxter's thoughts shifted from his ball game where bases were load-ed with no outs, to sounds from nearby roads announcing the possible arrival of his mother. Since it was Friday, he worried that John Rodgers might be picking him up rather than his mother which could mean that John and his moth-er would be going out for dinner, canceling the card game he sometimes had with his mother on Friday nights.

He stretched, no windup with men on base, and deliv-ered a fastball. He fielded the rebound successfully which meant there was one out. He now needed a double play to retire the side and win the game. His next pitch would be a slider, he thought. He stretched, looked at the imagi-nary base runner on third and was about to pitch when the black sedan with John Rodgers pulled up to the curb.

"Hi Tommy," came the voice from the car. "Your mom told me to pick you up. She'll be working late tonight."

"Sure," said Tommy, doing his best to conceal his disappointment. Slowly, he walked to the car, throwing his ball glove in the back seat. "Did she say when she'd be home?"

"Shouldn't be too late," came the reply. "We're supposed to go out to dinner tonight, though. Did you have a good day? What happened in school?"

"Nothing." The quiet answer on which Tommy rarely elaborated.

"Maybe there'll be a ball game on TV," said John, hoping to re-enliven the conversation.

"No, not tonight. Tomorrow."

It was apparent his passenger was not interested in talking, and John leaned forward to turn on the car radio. "Let's get the evening news," he said.

They rode without speaking, John flipping to various stations for news reports. A few lingering raindrops settled on the windshield as darkness enveloped the car. John was about to turn off the radio when a news report caught his attention.

"Did you hear that?" he said, turning up the volume on

the radio. "They think they may have caught the Sundown Dude."

"The what?" said Tommy

"Sundown Dude! A bank robber. They think it was a woman in disguise. Holding up a bank in Manhattan. It said she had a pistol. No bullets though. Apparently had it just to scare people during her robberies."

"No kidding," said Tommy. "The Sundown Dude was a woman?"

"Well, they haven't confirmed that," cautioned John. "They said the robber's hat and beard came off and that she had long blonde hair. They said it looked like a woman dressed as a man." John shook his head, pensively. The *Gazette* would have a field day with the copy. He wondered if Charlotte had heard the breaking news. It would make a good ending for her novel.

"Think she'll go to jail?" asked Tommy.

"No, she won't go to jail," said John. "She's dead. Shot!"

"Really?" said Tommy, his eyes widening at the news. "But how can the Sundown Dude be a woman?"

John leaned forward, turning off the radio where music had replaced the news. "Well, the radio just said that. Now, they're calling him the 'Sundown Doll.' 'But what's in a name? That which we call a rose by any other name would smell as sweet!' You know, Shakespeare."

"A baseball player?" said Tommy. "Did he play with the Yankees?"

"No, you're not there yet," said John, laughing slightly. "But when you're older, I'll tell you all about Shakespeare."

"Did you hear that?" said Tommy, sitting up quickly.

"Hear what?" asked John.

Tommy sat quietly, listening intently for a moment and then "I thought it was a motorcycle. Mom on her way somewhere. Guess not. But it sounded just like Mom. I know her Harley." Then hesitating, as though unsure of what he would say, he added, "Mom said maybe we're going to move in with you."

"She did?" Then after a pause, John added, "Yes, I hope so. Won't that be fun? We can watch baseball together."

Another moment of silence followed, and then Tommy spoke up, "You were talking about names. . . . After we move in with you, will I still call you John?"

John was quiet for a moment, then reached over with his free hand and patted the boy on the knee. "You can just call me whatever you'd like."

Tommy knew what he liked. All his buddies called their

father "Dad." But he hesitated. Maybe he should ask his mom first. She'd know best. But "Dad," that would be great.

He curled up in his seat staring ahead into the darkness, listening to the soothing hum of the engine.

"Dad!" he thought, relishing the word. "Just like the other guys."

"Wow!"

END

About the Author

Bernard F. Conners, former publisher of *The Paris Review*, has had a distinguished career in government, business, publishing, and film. He is the best-selling author of *Dancehall*, *Upper East Side Girl*, *Cruising with Kate*, *Tailspin*, *The Hampton Sisters*, and *Don't Embarrass the Bureau*. Mr. Conners lives in Loudonville, New York.